W9-CGM-616

THE GOALIE

BY

SUSAN SHREVE

BEECH TREE
NEW YORK

Copyright © 1996 by Susan Shreve
All rights reserved. No part of this book may be reproduced or
utilized in any form or by any means, electronic or mechanical, including
photocopying, recording, or by any information storage or retrieval system,
without permission in writing from the Publisher.

Inquiries should be addressed to Tambourine Books
a division of William Morrow & Company, Inc.
1350 Avenue of the Americas, New York, New York 10019.
www.williammorrow.com
Printed in the United States of America.

The text type is Veljovic Book.

The Library of Congress has cataloged the
Tambourine Books edition of *The Goalie* as follows:
Shreve, Susan Richards.
The goalie / by Susan Shreve.
p. cm.
Summary: Julie MacNeil feels threatened both in the family
and on the soccer field when her widower father
begins to date the mother of her arch-rival Benji True.
ISBN 0-688-14379-2
[1. Fathers and daughters—Fiction.   2. Widowers—Fiction.
3. Soccer—Fiction.]   I. Title.
PZ7.S55915Go 1996   [Fic]—dc20   96-17025   CIP AC

First Beech Tree Edition, 1998
ISBN 0-688-15858-7
10 9 8 7 6 5 4 3 2 1

To Paulette Kaufmann
with love and admiration,
and to all of the wonderful group
at Tambourine Books

Julie MacNeil was three the summer her mother was killed on Route 15 outside of Newtown where they lived. Julie, sitting in the backseat reading a pop-up book, was not hurt, and Tally, two months old and sleeping when the drunk driver plowed into the Chevrolet van, didn't even cry.

Julie remembered everything about that summer. At least she thought she did. Or else her memory was mixed in with her father's careful report of the details of the weeks after her mother's death. The way the house was always full of people, of relatives and friends and other children. The way her grandmother sat in the kitchen, rocking Tally and singing French lullabies. The way her aunt Melinda moved into the family room, sleeping on the couch, reading *Babar* or *Madeline* or Dr. Seuss. The way food kept appearing on the long table in the kitchen, although none of them was hungry.

Then, just after Julie's fourth birthday in September, the house emptied out. Her aunt, her grandmother, the visiting cousins, and other relatives went home to their own lives. And the small MacNeil family, Mr. MacNeil and Tally and Julie, their rag-doll cat Ernestine, and Monk, the blue-black lab puppy her aunt Melinda gave them to fill up the lonely house, settled into a new life.

But it wasn't really a new life. It was the same life with an empty space which had been Julie's mother, Alicia Mac-Neil, still forever in a silver frame on her old rolltop desk in the living room.

After the relatives left, they didn't talk about their mother. For weeks, Julie's father kept the picture of his wife on top of the desk and put the other photographs away.

"It's just us now, guys," he'd say to Julie and Tally. "You and me and Tally." And he'd give Julie a soft, joking punch on her arm, or wrestle her to the ground.

"Just you and us girls," Julie said to him one fall night just after the beginning of third grade. They were sitting at the kitchen table eating a frozen dinner, the kind of dinner they had when her father was tired, which happened often in the years after Alicia died.

"Do you ever wish I were a boy?" she asked.

"Nope, I don't wish you were a boy at all," he said. "I'm lucky you're a girl."

But in her heart Julie believed that he must long for a pal, a partner, a small cutout of himself, in the shape of an eight-year-old boy, instead of the reminder in Julie of his wife, with her dark olive skin and long strawberry-blond hair and dimpled smile.

"I'm good in sports," Julie said one night, washing up after dinner. "Some days I'm even better than the boys in my class."

"Even though you're smaller than they are?" her father asked.

"It doesn't matter how big I am," Julie replied. "I'm very fast."

"I certainly know you're fast," he said, patting her head. "I used to be pretty fast, too, before I got this belly."

It was autumn in Bucks County, a clear cool day, bright with the promise of winter, four years after her mother had died. She and her father, a tall, handsome, frumpy-looking man, who wore his clothes a little too large and his thick brown hair a little too long, were sitting at the picnic table in the garden. She was leaning against his shoulder, watching Tally run through the leaf piles, then fall facedown in them, her small arms spread out to embrace the world, Monk licking her pink hands.

Julie had an exact memory of the moment. She

remembered sitting at the picnic table in her blue Panther sweatshirt with the hood up, her high-tops, her hair braided too tight so it hurt the back of her head just enough to notice. She and her father were bragging back and forth about how they were fast runners and scrappy athletes and good losers, when suddenly Julie turned to him.

"You must be lonely without a friend your age at home," she said. "Like I have Tally."

"Sometimes," her father agreed.

"I can be everything, you know," she said.

"You are everything, chum," he said.

"I mean *really*," she said. "I can be your son and your daughter and your pal and sort of like your wife." She slid under his arm. "All those things in me."

"You really are all those things, Julie," her father said, giving her a soft panda-bear punch to the jaw.

Lately, she had been thinking about her mother's wedding ring. She had seen the wedding ring on top of her father's dresser. It was a small plain gold band that he kept in a wooden box with a picture of her mother and father on the beach, Alicia over her father's shoulders, her father running, probably toward the ocean to throw her in.

Julie wanted the ring. She didn't know why she wanted it, but she did. Unlike a lot of the girls in her third-grade class who wanted things—computer games and bicycles and ice skates and Rollerblades and dress-up clothes and Barbies— Julie only wanted three things: a black Panther baseball cap, fake eyeglasses from the five-and-ten like Aunt Melinda, and her mother's wedding ring.

On a slow walk with Tally and Monk along the river that afternoon, Julie asked her father if she could have the ring to wear.

"I don't think so," her father said thoughtfully. "That's the ring I gave to your mother, chum."

"I know, but I was thinking maybe I should have it now."

Her father shook his head. "It just doesn't feel right to me," he said.

He lifted her up in his arms, high above his head, and swung her upside down and over onto the ground.

"But ring or not, pal," he said, "you're still my everything."

So from the time she was eight years old, in third grade at Newtown Elementary, winter and summer vacation, Julie MacNeil became everything in the MacNeil house. She learned to cook, even dinners on evenings her father was home late from the radio station where he worked. She took care of Tally, who grew to be a round, yellow-haired munchkin of a little girl, slow to talk but with a happy temperament and a tendency to small disasters—falling down the front steps backward, falling frontward into the public swimming pool, falling into the toilet bowl, eating toadstools and baby aspirin and medicine for stomach flu.

There was a housekeeper called Bianca, whose job it was to take care of Tally, to get Julie off to school on time, to have dinner cooking when Jack MacNeil arrived home from work, to keep the house reasonably clean in spite of a black lab dirty from swims in the river and a fat cat who peed on the walls of the living room when she lost her temper.

But, according to Julie, Bianca was terrible at her job.

"I think we should fire Bianca," Julie said one evening at dinner with her father—baked potatoes she had made herself and cereal and chocolate-marshmallow ice cream. "She's not very good."

"What would we do if we fired Bianca, chum?" her father asked. "Who would take care of Tally when she comes home from nursery school, while you're still at school?"

"When Tally goes to kindergarten in September," Julie said, "I can do everything easily."

"I think we need some help, Julie. Even if your mother were alive we'd need help, and you're a busy girl with a lot of responsibility of your own."

"I can do it," Julie said. "Except the groceries, and we could do them on Sundays. Besides, all Bianca does is watch TV and call her boyfriend on the telephone." She shrugged.

"You know, chum, Bianca told me you're a little hard on her."

"Because she's not very good, Pops. She's a terrible cook," Julie said.

"She tells me you won't let her cook," her father said.

"I won't," Julie said, quite pleased with herself, "because

her food makes me sick. It makes Tally sick too. She threw up last night after the spaghetti."

"Well, try," her father said.

But Julie didn't want to try with Bianca. She wanted to run the MacNeil household by herself, to come home from school, make the dinner, play with Tally, read to her, and sit down at the dining room table for dinner with her father when he came home from work.

The problem with Bianca got worse and worse. On the first Monday of a new month, like clockwork, Bianca would arrive early in the morning with a sad face to say she was going to quit because Julie was "im-poss-eeble."

"Please, Bianca," Jack MacNeil would beg. "Give us one more month. I promise Julie will be better."

And he'd give Bianca just a bit more money to encourage her. But he could never keep his promise about Julie.

"Tally wouldn't have gone down to the river if Bianca had been watching carefully," Julie said one night at a dinner she had cooked of pancakes and hot chocolate and runny banana pudding made from a box. "And when she ate the toadstool, she was out in the garden alone."

"How do you know she was in the garden alone if you were at school, chum?" her father asked.

"I know because Tally told me," Julie said.

"That is not what Tally told me."

"Well, maybe Bianca was in the garden," Julie said, looking off in the distance, "but she was probably reading one of those magazines she likes to read full of women's clothes."

During one of her summer visits, Aunt Melinda made a particular point to take Julie out to lunch at Freezie's Ice Cream Shop for a private conversation.

"Sweetheart, you've got to go easy on Bianca," she said. "I know she's not your favorite, but she's better than nothing."

"She's an idiot," Julie said. "I even make the beds myself. She only pretends to wash the sheets. We sleep in sheets which have been dirty for a year. She doesn't like Monk and she doesn't like Ernestine and she doesn't like me."

"But you're safe and Tally's safe and your father doesn't have to worry all day while he's doing his radio program."

"He should worry, Aunt Melinda," Julie said. "We wouldn't be safe at all if I weren't here."

"I don't know, sweet pea. You're not exactly grown-up yet," Aunt Melinda said. "Maybe you and Tally should come to live with me in Philadelphia for a while till you get a little older."

"I can't," Julie said. "Daddy would fall to pieces without us."

There was no fighting with Julie. She was right on the subject of her father and on the subject of Bianca and absolutely certain she could do a better job running the MacNeil house alone.

But Bianca had stayed through Julie's eighth and ninth

years and Tally's fourth and fifth years until the middle of September, six years after their mother had died.

When Bianca threatened to quit this time, Jack MacNeil didn't beg her to stay. He didn't offer her a little more money, and he didn't promise her that Julie would be less difficult when she turned ten.

So on the second Tuesday in September, Bianca left without a word. And Julie's father did not mention finding a replacement.

That night after practicing soccer and reading to Tally and finishing her homework in math and writing a story for language arts called "Bad Bad Bianca Boo-hoo," Julie wandered into her father's bedroom, where he was on the telephone.

"I'll be right with you, chum," he said, telling the person on the other line he would call back.

Julie crawled into his bed.

"Aren't you happy?" she said to him.

"Very happy," he said.

"Things are going to be so much better with just us," Julie said.

"I think you're right. I don't know what I'd do without you," her father said, boxing her gently on the chin. "You know what a goalie does in soccer, chum?" he asked.

"Of course," Julie said. "That's the position I want to play."

"Well you're our goalie, Jules. The MacNeil family personal goalie."

"What does that mean?" Julie asked.

"That means you protect me and Tally and Monk and Ernestine from outside trouble," her father said.

And Julie laughed.

That night she slept the sweetest sleep she could remember with Monk and Ernestine and Quacker, the stuffed duck her mother had given her before she died. She got up early, before dawn, dressed in her best jeans and shirt, and made waffles with strawberries and orange juice and coffee for Jack MacNeil. "Yum," Tally said.

"My favorite," her father said. "Thank you, chum."

"I'll cook breakfast every morning," Julie said, "since it's just us. Together forever."

"I hope things stay like they are," Tally said wistfully as they walked to school.

"They will," Julie said full of confidence, full of her new importance as the mother in the family, full of pleasure and happiness and high spirits. "Besides, nothing could be worse than Bianca, and she's gone."

"I guess," Tally said.

But as it turned out, things could be worse than Bianca. And they were.

The following afternoon when Julie got home from school with Tally after drama class and soccer, after a trip to the drugstore for M&M's, after walking Monk and picking up milk and cereal at the 7-Eleven, there was a note on the kitchen table from their father.

Dear Julie and Tally,

I have a surprise for tonight. My friend Eliza True, whom you both will love, and her son Benji, just Julie's age, are coming for dinner. I'm bringing in takeout so you won't have to cook, chum, and will be home about seven.

Love to my troops,

Pops

"Do you know those people?" Tally asked.

"I don't," Julie said.

"Have you ever heard of them?"

"Nope," Julie said.

"Me neither."

"But I think Daddy's wrong about one thing," Julie said.

"About what?" Tally asked, taking out a box of chocolate chip cookies for a snack.

"I don't think we're going to love Eliza True," she said.

"How come?" Tally asked.

"I just don't think we will," Julie said.

Julie threw the note in the wastebasket, went upstairs to her bedroom, closed the door, and sat down on the end of her bed. She could hear Tally running up the stairs behind her and Monk galloping down the hall, but she wasn't in the mood for conversation.

"Julie?" Tally said through the crack in the door.

"You can't come in," Julie said firmly.

She could hear Tally making the funny little sounds she made in her throat when she was planning to cry.

"Julie?" Tally called again.

"I'm thinking, Tal," Julie said.

"Me too," Tally said. "I'm thinking I hate you."

"We're not allowed to say hate, Tally," Julie said automatically. Ever since she had taken over the job of mother, she had considered herself responsible for Tally's discipline if her father wasn't at home.

"I can't help it," Tally said crossly. "Because I do hate you."

Julie heard Tally stamp across the hall and slam the door to her bedroom. Julie lay back on her bed and looked at the ceiling. Her first thought was to call Eliza True, if she could find her number in the telephone book, to tell her not to come to dinner with her stupid son because the MacNeil family was suddenly ill with blue-coated strep throat.

Or she could go to a hotel. There was a very nice hotel in New Hope where her grandmother stayed when she came to visit, because she was allergic to Monk and Ernestine and couldn't spend the night at the MacNeils' house. But that was complicated because she'd have to take Monk on a leash and Ernestine in her box, and Tally would pee in the hotel bed, which is what she did whenever she slept in a strange place.

Maybe she should call Aunt Melinda.

"She can't come to my house with her idiot son," Julie said to Melinda when her aunt, out of breath from running up the stairs to her apartment, answered the phone.

"Oh, Jules. Don't be so fierce. The son may not turn out to be an idiot," Melinda said. "You might even like him."

"Not a chance," Julie said. "I think I already know him from school."

And then she added for good measure, "I think he's the one in sixth grade who does drugs."

"I doubt he's on drugs, Julie," Melinda said. "I think you're making too much of this, sweet pea. Your father has invited a friend to dinner for one night. You don't have to marry her," Melinda said. "In fact, she may never come back."

"She won't," Julie said. "I promise you she won't."

There was a long sigh on the other end of the phone.

"Try, Jules," Melinda said. "Just swallow hard and try."

"I do try, Aunt Melinda. I try a lot, but it's very hard," Julie said, a new thought slipping into her mind, "I don't think my mother would like to have Eliza True here for dinner."

"Your mother . . ." Melinda began.

Julie knew she was about to say what she always said—that Alicia MacNeil had been dead for six years and it was terrible and sad, but Julie and her father and Tally had to make a new life.

"You're a tough one, Julia MacNeil," Aunt Melinda said.

"I know," Julie said, "but I sort of have to be tough with the job I have to do."

She lay back down on her bed, lifted Ernestine beside her, and considered her plans. She must do something. If her mother's house was threatened by strangers, it was Julie's job to protect it.

In pictures, Alicia MacNeil was a pretty woman with long hair she wore pulled back in a low ponytail and sparkling eyes. Julie remembered her eyes. She remembered the feel of her mother in the room and the sound of her voice, which was low and gravelly—she had heard it on tape. She remembered tiny moments. Her mother's bare feet at the end of the bed when they were reading a story; the tickle of her hair when she carried Julie to the ocean one summer at the beach; the last time she saw her face to face, as Alicia MacNeil fastened the seatbelt of Julie's car seat on the drive to the market that would end in the accident that took her life.

But she didn't remember her mother exactly. Sometimes she held the picture from the rolltop desk next to her own face and looked in the mirror. They looked similar, her features less distinct than her mother's, but familiar. She imagined that when she was older she would look like Alicia, that people like Melinda and her father and her grandmother would exclaim, "Oh, Julie, you have come to look so much like her."

And that would give Julie a sense of accomplishment, of responsibility for the look she had achieved, for igniting her mother's memory in the people who had loved her.

Julie longed for a mother. Sometimes, especially at school, she was embarrassed not to have a mother, as if she were somehow accountable. But because she could only remember patches of their lives together, she didn't really miss her own mother. Not enough. Not as much as she should. She worried about that. Lying awake in the dark, thinking of what responsibilities she had for the next day—taking Tally to the doctor for an allergy shot and shopping at the drugstore for toothpaste and shampoo and dog food for Monk—she would imagine what it would be like if her mother were still alive, and she would try to recapture Alicia MacNeil on the screen of her memory.

This afternoon, as the day moved toward evening and the arrival of Eliza True with her stupid son, she *was* thinking about her mother.

And she knew exactly what she had to do.

Tally was crying when Julie knocked on her bedroom door.

"I hate you," she called out.

"I know," Julie said gently.

"So does Monk. Worse than me," Tally said. "He thinks you're a creep."

"I'm sorry, Tal," Julie said.

There was a long silence, a little breathy cry.

"C'n I come in?" Julie asked.

"Maybe," Tally said.

"Please?" Julie asked. "I know I was mean to you."

Tally was sitting with Monk on her bed, painting his toenails with magenta nail polish.

"He might lick it and get sick," Julie said.

"I'm not letting him lick it," Tally said. "He likes to wear nail polish."

Julie didn't argue. She didn't even get angry when the nail polish spilled on the bed and they had to turn over Tally's comforter so the magenta splotch wouldn't show.

"I was thinking," Julie said, sitting down on the bed next to Tally. "We have almost no pictures of Mommy around the house except the one on the desk in the living room and the one in the kitchen with me and you the year you were born."

Tally was holding Monk's painted paw, waiting for it to dry.

"I think we should go through the photographs and put some up around the house," Julie said.

"Maybe in the kitchen to cover the yucky yellow walls?" Tally asked.

"Everywhere. Lots of them. All over the kitchen and the living room and the dining room."

"Do you think Daddy will like that?"

"Of course. He'll love it," she said. "He loved her very very much."

"I know," Tally said, scrambling down from the bed, following Julie downstairs to the dining room where the photographs, hundreds of them, were kept in albums and boxes and cardboard containers. They sat on the floor side by side with the albums in front of them.

"How many should we choose?" Tally asked.

"Zillions," Julie said, pulling out the boxes of photographs.

"But we don't have any frames for them," Tally said. "How can we make them stand up?"

"We'll just Scotch Tape them, sort of roll the tape on the back of the pictures and stick them all over the wall," Julie said.

She opened the boxes and took out the envelopes of photographs.

"How come we're doing this today?" Tally asked. "I thought you were going to help me with my Native American project."

"We need to do it today," Julie said. "Tonight after dinner, I'll help you with your project."

"I need to make a village," Tally was saying. "I hope we have paste and crayons."

"We do," Julie said absently.

"And construction paper?"

"We do."

"You're not listening to me, Julie," Tally said.

Julie wasn't listening. She was imagining the walls full of pictures of their mother. Imagining Eliza True walking through the front door, and there on the walls of the front hall and in the kitchen and the dining room and the living room, every place she went, was picture after picture of Alicia MacNeil.

The first set of pictures were taken when their mother was young, maybe in high school, pictures with their father in a football uniform, their mother in blue jeans and a big white sweater, her arm around their father, laughing.

"They met in high school," Julie said. "Aunt Melinda told me that. They went to the same high school and Daddy played football and Mommy played field hockey and they started to go out with each other when they were fifteen."

There were pictures from a prom—their mother bright-cheeked in pale lipstick and a long strapless white dress, their father young and pimply faced in his tuxedo with a white flower in the lapel, his long lazy hair falling over one eye. There were pictures at the ocean, their mother in a tiny bikini, their father skinny and with slicked-back hair playing volleyball on the beach. Pictures in college at the University of Vermont, where they both went to school, ice-skating in matching bright blue parkas, skiing, sitting on a long sled, their father's arms wrapped around their mother, a gray snowy picture in which they were leaning toward each other, almost the same height, kissing.

"She was so pretty," Tally said happily, making Scotch Tape circles on the backs of the pictures.

"We are very lucky to be her daughters." Julie said, feeling triumphant.

"She was nice too?" Tally asked.

"She was wonderful," Julie said.

The wedding pictures were in the second box. The wedding took place in the summer in Bryn Mawr, Pennsylvania, outside of Philadelphia. Their mother wore a long white dress, her strawberry-blond hair laced with tiny white flowers, their father young and handsome in a suit with long black tails. They were married in a stone church—Aunt Melinda was there and their grandparents, and a lot of other people Julie had never met. There were pictures of the party, mainly dancing pictures; her mother and father; her mother and the grandfather who died before Julie was born; pictures of her parents cutting the tall wedding cake decorated with roses; and a large, beautiful framed picture of Alicia MacNeil in her wedding dress looking away from the camera.

Julie taped a newspaper article from the Philadelphia paper announcing the marriage of Alicia Carolina DuPres and John Joseph MacNeil on July 1, 1985, to the bottom corner of the frame, and put a tiny nail in the wall of the front hall so that when Eliza True arrived through the front, the first thing she saw would be their mother.

"Are you sure Daddy's going to be happy we're doing this?" Tally asked.

"Of course he'll be happy," Julie said, taking out photographs of Alicia pregnant. "He loved her."

By six o'clock in the afternoon, just the beginning of dusk, the late afternoon light filtering through the MacNeil's cheerful house, the walls of the downstairs were plastered with pictures of their mother. Wedding pictures in the hall, high school and college pictures in the living room, pregnant pictures and baby pictures with Julie and Tally in the kitchen, vacation pictures at the beach and in Mexico and in Vermont all over the dining room, family pictures everywhere.

"Daddy likes things sort of orderly," Tally said concerned.

"This is orderly, Tal," Julie said. "Don't worry."

At seven, the telephone rang, and it was Jack MacNeil.

"I'm picking up Chinese food at Hunan Gallery, chum," he said. "Then I'll be home."

"What about your friends?" Julie asked.

"Oh, I'm picking them up too." Her father was in high spirits. "We'll be there at seven-thirty. Maybe you could set the table for five."

"Are we going to get dressed up?" Tally asked.

"Nope," Julie said. "We should look normal."

"But maybe we should set the table," Tally said.

"You can do that, Tal," Julie said. "I need to start my homework."

"I'm not so good at setting the table," Tally said.

"That's okay," Julie said. "You're good enough."

Julie went to her room carrying a complaining Ernestine, turned on the light at her desk, took her math book out of her book bag, and started her homework.

She heard her father's car pull down the long driveway and stop beside the house. She heard the front door open and the sounds of chatter in the downstairs hall, but she didn't get up. And then she heard the thump, thump of Tally's sneakers on the stairs.

"They're here," Tally said.

"I know," Julie said. "I heard them."

"The boy's here too. He goes to your school. He says he knows you."

"I don't know him."

"Yes, you do," Tally said. "His name is Benji True, and he plays soccer with you."

"I do know him," Julie said quietly. "He's a creep."

She knew Benji perfectly well. She simply had not known his last name. Just that afternoon, in fact, she had sat next to him on the bench for soccer tryouts.

She'd heard about Benji True, that he'd moved with his mother from Connecticut and was a grade ahead with a reputation for being loud. She had not liked him from the start.

"Are you trying out for the team?" he'd asked. He was a little shorter than she was and square, with curly beige hair and a crackly voice.

Julie nodded.

"I didn't think they had girls here."

"Sometimes they do," she said.

"They didn't last year. I saw the team picture," Benji said.

Julie shrugged. "Some years they don't."

"What position are you trying for?" Benji asked.

"I'm not sure yet," Julie said, unwilling to say anything about her hopes for herself.

"I'm trying out for goalie," Benji True said, turning his baseball cap backward, taking out a stick of gum. "I'm not bad. I played goalie for my old school in Connecticut."

Julie's heart fell. She leaned forward, resting her chin in her hands, waiting for Coach Harrison, a large chunky man with carrot-colored hair that he wore very short and enormous hands.

"Is anybody else trying out for goalie?" Benji asked.

"I don't know," Julie replied. "Maybe Tom Boyle."

Goalie was Julie's position. She had planned for it for two years, since just after second grade when the junior soccer coach told her she was good enough to play with the boys. She had practiced for it all summer before fifth grade, morning and night on the high-school football field playing with her father, or else, when he was working, practicing alone in the backyard.

She had played soccer for the county since she was five, and most years she made the first team. When she was in first grade, she was faster than any of the boys, and although she was not particularly good at scoring goals, she played offense because she was quick and good with her feet.

"Pretty good with your feet," her father said when they practiced together on the high-school field. They practiced often; evenings until the days got too short in the fall, and all spring after the rains stopped in late April.

* * *

By the time she was in the third grade, she was no longer faster than all of the boys. She was faster than some of them, and by the fourth grade, she placed in the middle in coed races. Faster than all of the girls but Andrea, faster than half of the boys.

"It's not fair," she had said to her father.

"Choose a position for your skills," her father said. "You're quick and shifty. You're good with your hands, and you're pure courage."

"What position is good for my skills?" she'd asked him. "Defense?"

"Defense is exactly right," he had said.

"Maybe goalie?"

"You'd be a great goalie," her father said.

"I don't know about my chances for being a goalie on a mostly boys' team," Julie said. "It's sort of the most important position."

"Why not? You're good under pressure," her father said. "Go for it, chum."

Downstairs, Julie heard her father calling, heard the rattle of dishes, the clinking of silverware, the cheerful chatter of voices.

"Jules," he said, "Come on downstairs, chum. Dinner's on."

Julie closed her math book.

"Coming," she called, picking up Ernestine, "in just a second."

* * *

She turned out her light, walked down the hall to her father's room, opened the box on top of the dresser, took out the gold band he had given her mother on the day of their wedding, and put it on her thumb.

Julie slipped into her chair next to her father, across from Eliza True, and next to Tally, who was jabbering happily.

The table had been set with paper towels instead of napkins, and the Chinese dinner was in cardboard containers in the middle.

"We have napkins," Julie said solemnly, putting a piece of paper towel in her lap, glancing over at Eliza True.

She was a tall woman with dark hair, which she wore short, and a sharp-featured, tannish face, a little like their mother's face. But she was not nearly as pretty, Julie thought. And her long-fingered hands, when Julie shook them, were cold.

"I couldn't find the napkins, chum," her father said, passing her the containers of chicken with water chestnuts, and wonton soup, and egg rolls, and beef with snow peas.

"I don't eat Chinese food," Julie said, folding her hands in her lap.

"You used to eat it," Tally said cheerfully. "We have it at Aunt Melinda's all the time."

"That's before I knew I was allergic to monosodium glutamate," Julie said quietly.

Tally looked at her dinner.

"In the Chinese food?" Tally asked. "Maybe I'm allergic too," she said.

"We studied monosodium glutamate in science this week," Benji said.

"I don't think you are allergic, Julie," Jack MacNeil said.

"Wrong," Julie said under her breath. "Anyway"—she gave Tally a small suggestive kick under the table—"I'm not very hungry since I had the stomach flu last night."

Tally looked up.

"Me too," she said.

Julie imagined herself orphaned, forced to sit with this man who called himself her father, this cold-fingered woman, and her dreadful son.

She was planning her escape. She would take Tally and very little luggage. And they'd have to leave soon, before Tally was brainwashed by this woman and her son, wrongly believing them kind and agreeable people. She'd take Monk and Ernestine, and they'd travel by taxicab to Aunt Melinda's. Perhaps they'd move to Aunt Melinda's permanently.

31

"I understand you and Benji know each other from soccer," Jack MacNeil was saying.

"We met yesterday," Benji True said. "She's the only girl trying out for the soccer team."

"I haven't decided if I'm trying out yet," Julie said.

"Of course you're trying out, chum," her father said. "You're a wonderful athlete."

"The coach says she's good for a girl," Benji said, busy picking the snow peas out of the beef sauce.

"Benjamin," Eliza True said.

Benji shrugged. "I'm only repeating what the coach said."

"I'm sure Julie is a terrific athlete whether or not she's a girl," Eliza True said. "An athlete is an athlete."

Julie could feel her face reddening to the color of bright cooked beets, the hot blood on the surface of her skin, her heart fluttering, her eyes beginning to burn. She was certainly not going to allow herself to cry, she thought, opening her eyes very wide, looking directly at Eliza True, who was eating her egg roll with her fingers. She had very long teeth.

"So what position are you trying out for, Benji?" Jack MacNeil asked, slipping Monk the rest of his egg roll. "Center forward? You look like a center forward to me."

Benji shook his head.

"Goalie," he said. "I've always played goalie."

"Goalie?" Tally asked, full of excitement, and before Julie had a chance to kick her under the table again, she had already said, "Julie's trying out for goalie too."

"Actually I've changed my mind," Julie said coolly. "I'm not trying out for goalie."

"'S'okay with me if you try out for goalie," Benji said. "I mean if that's what you're worried about."

"I'm not worried," Julie said. "I'm just not trying out for goalie."

"I thought you were," Tally said. "I thought that's what you'd been working on with Daddy all summer."

"I think you misunderstood, Tally," Julie said. "Daddy has been trying to get in shape. I've just been helping him out."

"Julie and I like to kick a ball around together," Jack MacNeil said quietly. "And she's played soccer for a Bucks County league since she was small."

"I hope you do try out, Julie," Eliza True said. "I like it when a girl has the courage to try out for a team dominated by boys."

After dinner, they sat in the living room in dim light, surrounded by the walls of pictures of Alicia MacNeil. Julie sat on a large chair with Ernestine, who had arrived from the garden with a dead mouse and sat proudly licking her paws. Tally sat on her father's lap across from Eliza True, who sat in a straight-back chair with her long, thin legs crossed.

"Is that your Mom all over the wall?" Benji asked, lying on his stomach on the floor with a comic.

Julie glanced at her father, but he had no particular expression on his face.

"Yes, it is," she said.

"We put them up today," Tally said.

"That's not exactly true, Tal." Julie shot her sister a fierce look. "They've been up forever."

"I mean we put up a couple of new ones today," Tally said.

"She was lovely," Eliza True said later to Julie, as they stood in the hall ready to leave.

"Yes, she was," Julie said, holding Ernestine over her shoulder, leaning against the front door. "And very athletic," she added.

"No wonder you're an athlete, then," Eliza True said.

"What made you think your mother was athletic?" Jack MacNeil asked later, when he came into Julie's bedroom to tell her good night.

"I guessed she was athletic," Julie said. "In a lot of the pictures, she's playing hockey or skiing or sledding or swimming," she said coolly, continuing to read *Charlotte's Web*.

Her father sat down at the end of her bed.

"Well, you're right. She was a very good athlete. I just had never talked about that with you."

"I know all about my mother," Julie said. "I've made a study of her."

Her father shook his head sadly.

"I don't know what to say, chum."

"About what?"

"About what happened tonight."

"It was a perfectly normal night," Julie said.

"Not exactly," her father said.

"What wasn't normal, except we usually don't have dinner with people from your work?" Julie asked.

"I think you made too much of Eliza coming over."

"Like what?" Julie asked. "I made nothing of it. She's okay. She's sort of skinny and sickly-looking but okay. Benji told me she has some kind of disease which is why she's so skinny." She stretched, raising her arms high above her head as if the whole conversation was boring her to death. "Heart disease, I think he said."

"What are you talking about, Julie?"

He turned on the overhead light.

"But who knows what to believe from Benji?" She put *Charlotte's Web* facedown on the bed. "I suppose you could tell he has a little bit of a drug problem."

"I could tell nothing about a drug problem," her father said crossly. "It's risky to tell tales on other people, chum, and I think you have too much imagination about the Trues. They're just ordinary people."

Julie shrugged. "It's none of my business, of course."

"If this is because of the goalie conversation at dinner, I'm sorry," her father began. "I know that upset you."

"Wrong," Julie said. "I wasn't at all upset about the goalie position. I was only trying out for the soccer team because you wanted me to, anyway," she said. "I sort of hate soccer."

"I don't know what to believe and what not to believe with you tonight." Her father took hold of her foot under the covers.

"Well, you can believe that some people in the sixth grade told me on the playground that Benji used drugs in Connecticut before he moved here."

"He doesn't seem at all the type," her father said, standing beside her bed, his arms folded across his chest.

"I'm just telling you what I heard," she said.

"Well, Julie . . ." her father said, looking away out the window toward the garden where a storm was picking up, the wind bending the trees like dancers away from the house.

"Don't worry about it, Daddy."

"I'm not worried," Jack MacNeil said. "I just wanted to talk about tonight."

"I don't want to talk about tonight," Julie said. "I'm behind in school and have to finish this book for tomorrow."

He seemed suddenly very old to her as he kissed the top of her head and turned off the light.

"Good night, sweetheart," he said. "I know it's been hard for you."

"Daddy?"

"Yes?"

"Don't take the pictures down."

"Pictures?"

"You know."

"Of course I won't, chum," he said.

When he left, she closed *Charlotte's Web*, turned off the light beside her bed, put Ernestine under the covers, patted the bed for Monk to hop up beside her, and sat up in the dark, looking at the gold ring glittering in the moonlight on her thumb.

If her father had seen the ring, she thought, he'd decided not to mention it to her.

In the mornings, Julie and Tally met Lila O'Shee at the corner of Route 7 and Newtown Road at seven forty-five. Usually Lila was the first to arrive and had already eaten her snack and half her lunch by the time Julie and Tally came around the corner. But this morning Lila wasn't there.

Lila O'Shee had been Julie's closest friend since birth. According to Julie's father, Julie and Lila spent their afternoons together in the same playpen. She was a tall and long-legged girl, who looked like the expensive kind of baby doll with soft hair and beautifully painted cheeks. Everyone in the fifth grade loved her. But Julie was Lila's favorite.

She lived behind the MacNeils in a small cottage on a few acres of hilly land with a large barn. Julie used to spend time in the barn playing in the hay with Lila or with the barn kittens born in triples every season, or crawling along the rafters, or kicking a soccer ball back and forth from one end of the huge barn floor to the other, or swinging on a long rope from the loft to the ground. But, by third grade, when Julie took over the role of *everything* in the MacNeil family, she didn't have time after school to go to the O'Shees.

"I don't understand," Lila said. "You could bring Tally with you. I could help you look after her."

"I have too much to do at home," Julie said. "Tally has lessons or I have to go to the drugstore or buy the groceries for dinner. I'm just too busy to play any longer."

"It's pretty dumb to me," Lila had said. "Soon enough you'll be grown-up, and it'll be too late. That's what my mother says."

Julie had shrugged.

"My father needs me too much," she said.

"You're indispensible," her father told her often. "I don't know what I would do without you."

Julie believed him, and it felt wonderful to be indispensible. She was so busy that she didn't even miss the afternoons in the O'Shee barn. But Lila missed them and was always a little angry at Julie.

"I suppose I'll have to get a new best friend," Lila said.

And eventually she did. Sometimes walking home from school with Lila and one of her new best friends, Mary or Pamela or Sally or Beatrice, Julie would feel a terrible sadness as she watched them go off in the direction of the O'Shees' barn, arm in arm, chattering happily. But then she and Tally would take Monk to the river, and she'd help Tally do her homework, and make dessert for their father, and Julie would forget all about Lila and her new best friends.

At school however, they were still the closest of friends, always together, equals—good in sports, good in English, bad in math, good in music, bad in art, good at skating and soccer, bad at swimming, well-liked by the boys, too much of a tomboy for some of the girls. On weekends when her father was at home, Julie went out with her friends. She and Lila were invited to the same birthday parties, the same sleep overs, the same movie afternoons. They were both tall and leggy for their age, with long dark hair, and slender, even skinny, with dimples—Lila had two on either corner of her lips, and Julie had a large, deep dimple in her cheek and a cleft in her chin. People who didn't know them thought they might be sisters, sometimes even twins, not identical, but enough alike to have come from the same mother at the same time. Which is why they were sometimes enemies. They were alike. But not exactly.

So when Lila got an A in her Native American project, Julie got an A–, and when Lila got the lead in *Annie*, Julie got the role of secretary, and when Julie made first-string county soccer playing offense, Lila made second-string. And each time one or the other of them was a little jealous.

They started out friends because of their mothers. That much Julie knew. But she had never volunteered a conversation about her mother with Mrs. O'Shee. In fact the last time Mrs.O'Shee mentioned Alicia MacNeil, sitting at dinner in the O'Shees' backyard, Julie had suddenly gone silent and called her father to pick her up because she was feeling sick.

In a way Julie did not entirely understand, she felt like a failure with Lila because her own mother was dead—as though she were somehow responsible for her mother's absence.

"We're going to be so late," Tally said. "I want to go on without Lila."

"She'll be here, I promise," Julie said. "We won't be late."

But when Lila finally arrived at the corner of Route 7 and Newtown Road, running down the path, her book bag flying behind her, it was almost eight o'clock.

"We've got to hurry," Tally said. "I'll be in trouble."

"I'm sorry," Lila said, falling in step beside them as they hurried down the road. "I was having a long talk with my mother and didn't even realize how late it was."

She pulled a box of granola cookies from her book bag and passed them to Julie. "Are you trying out for goalie?" Lila asked. "Your father told my father you'd been practicing all summer while I was away at camp."

"I don't know. I haven't decided," Julie said. "I went to tryouts yesterday."

"The trouble is there's a new boy called Benji who's trying out for goalie," Tally said. "He's very good, or else he says he's very good. Which one?" She looked over at Julie.

"Who knows?" Julie said. "I haven't seen him play."

"Benji True?" Lila asked. "The new boy in sixth grade?"

"Have you met him?" Julie asked.

"I met him," Lila said. "He was at church on Sunday, and I see him on the playground."

"Well, he's a creep," Julie said.

They were walking along Newtown Road just across from the elementary school, where they could hear the bell ringing for homeroom and see the students hurrying toward the doors. They stopped at the corner to cross the street with the crossing guard.

"It's too bad he's a creep," Lila said, "'cause Mama told me this morning that his mother is your father's girlfriend." She said it kindly, as if Julie already knew.

But Julie's heart flew into her mouth, and her blood rushed to her face, and her teeth clenched to breaking. She was so angry, she thought she was going to cry right there in front of Lila and Tally and the crossing guard.

"My father doesn't have a girlfriend," Julie said, catching her breath, walking across the street.

"I thought he liked Benji's mother." Lila shrugged. "My mother says she's nice."

"She's not so nice," Julie said evenly.

"She's a little nice, Julie," Tally said.

"Wrong," Julie said.

"She came for dinner last night," Tally said. "We had Chinese food with monosodium something or other."

"My father just feels sorry for her because she's divorced," Julie said. "But she's not my father's girlfriend at all."

"I guess my mother was wrong," Lila said quietly.

"She was," Julie said, walking up the side steps of Newtown Elementary. "She was completely wrong."

"But it would be sort of nice if your father had a girlfriend," Lila said tentatively. "That's what my mother says."

"My father is totally happy with just us. He told me he never wants a girlfriend," Julie said, turning into the school office, telling Lila she had something to check on in the office and would meet her in class.

"I have to make a telephone call," she said to the secretary.

"You'll be late for homeroom," the secretary said.

"I can't help it," Julie said. "It's an emergency."

Jack MacNeil was a newscaster at a radio station in Doylestown with a talk show called *The Jack MacNeil Show* broadcast nationally by National Public Radio. First thing in the morning he did the news; the local news and then the national news. Each day he had a guest whom he interviewed by telephone or sometimes in person. *The Jack MacNeil Show* was on the air from eleven A.M. to noon.

Once a year, he took Julie and Tally with him to see what he did all day. Every day, he told them, it was the same. He got to the office at seven-thirty, had coffee with milk and sugar and a cinnamon-raisin bagel, read the newspaper, looked at the printout copy of the daily news, and practiced saying the news or the weather before he was on the air. "The weather in southeastern Pennsylvania will be warm and sunny today with clouds beginning in the late afternoon. . . ."

Or, "Good morning, this is Jack MacNeil. A bomb exploded on a bus in Tel Aviv this morning, injuring twenty-six."

After the news, he met his guest for the day a few minutes before the show went on the air, so the microphones could be tested for the broadcast. After the show, he met with his staff to decide on the guests for the next week, then he went to lunch with Tim Crane, the engineer for his program, or one of his guests. And in the afternoon, he sat in his office and made up the questions to ask his guest for the following day. At five o'clock, he did the evening news and then rushed home to be with his daughters.

That was his day every day, exactly the same, and Julie always knew what he was doing and where to reach him.

Except today.

When she called, Annette, the switchboard operator, said he had come in as usual but she didn't know where he was.

"Having coffee in his office," Julie said with certainty. "Reading the newspaper."

But today, he wasn't there.

In fact, according to Annette, the newspaper wasn't at his desk and someone in the office said he had gone out for coffee.

"With whom?" Julie asked.

But Annette had no idea.

"Tell him . . ." Julie began. She was going to say it was an emergency, and it was. But she changed her mind. "Tell him that Tally and I might be moving to Philadelphia soon."

And she hung up.

* * *

On the way to class, she passed Benji True at his locker.

"My mom tells me I'm supposed to say I'm sorry," he said.

"Sorry for what?" Julie asked coolly.

"Sorry for the stuff I said about you being a girl and an athlete. That sort of stuff."

"I didn't even notice," Julie said, going into the classroom, shutting the door behind her.

When she arrived, math class had started. Lila had saved her a seat.

"Coach Harrison came in while you were out," Lila said. "Tryouts are at two-thirty this afternoon, and you should get there early."

"I changed my mind about trying out," Julie said, sliding down in her seat so Mr. Able, writing fractions on the chalkboard, couldn't see her. She took out her math book and flipped through the pages. Between pages 46 and 47, where she had been doing her homework the night before, was a note from her father written in red pen:

Listen to me, Ms. Everything, just this once.
Don't give up being goalie.
You're all heart, which is another word for courage.
Just like your mother.
> *Love,*
> *Your Pops*

* * *

And in spite of herself, in spite of the great worry and sadness spreading across her life since Eliza True appeared at her house, Julie MacNeil smiled.

All last summer, Julie had practiced playing goalie with her father. They got up early with the sun, had breakfast on the screened porch overlooking the garden and the long path to the river, and then, with Tally and Monk, they biked along the river to the large field behind the high school for practice.

Jack and Tally kicked, and Julie, standing in a makeshift goal, blocked the balls. She got very good. By August, she was blocking all of Tally's shots and many of her father's. By the time school started, she was almost certain that she'd be chosen goalie. Tucker Ryan would try out, of course. Probably Terry Winner, who was good enough but not dependable, and maybe Beth Jones. But in early September, before she heard of Benji True, Julie was confident. She had daydreams in which she saw herself in knee pads and chest pads, her baseball cap on bill backward, her face guard disguising her expression, her arms extended to a ball spiraling toward her, almost out of reach, and, miraculously, she'd catch it.

Julie met Lila on the hill overlooking the soccer field, and together, they watched the boys dragging their equipment to tryouts. It was a lovely September day, warm and breezy with the smell of autumn in the air but the ground still warm enough to lie on without a chill.

"Do you think you're the only girl trying out?" Lila asked. She had come with Julie for "moral support" as she put it.

"Beth Jones, maybe," Julie said.

"No one else?"

"I haven't heard of anybody else," Julie said.

"It's too bad there isn't a girls' team," Lila said.

"I wouldn't want to be on it," Julie said.

"Well," Lila said, lying back in the grass. "I would hate to be on a boys' team." She stretched her arms over her head. "Boys smell so awful, especially their feet."

Julie laughed.

In the distance the coach was walking across the field with one of the players, dragging his net full of soccer balls.

"Is that who I think it is?" Julie asked.

"Benji True," Lila said.

Julie squinted.

"Creep," she said, burying her head in her hands so he wouldn't see her.

"He sees you, Jules," Lila said.

"Great."

"He's on his way over," Lila said.

"Double great," Julie said

Benji dashed up the hill and crashed down between them.

"Hiya," he said. "I'm glad you changed your mind, Julie."

He rolled over on his back. "My mother said if you decided not to try out because of me, I was going to be in big trouble."

"You couldn't make me change my mind, Benji." The coach called for some laps around the track and Julie jumped up.

"Stretch out," the coach called. "Then take four laps."

"Run with me," Benji said. "You can keep up."

"Of course I can keep up," Julie said.

She started around the track on the outside lane, in pace with Benji and the other boys. She was conscious of where Benji was running. She could feel him just behind her, two lanes over, even though she didn't turn to look. But she had a sense that he could run much faster, that he was holding back to stay even with her, that his ordinary pace was longer, that he was a real athlete. It made her tired just to think of him.

She fell back two paces behind some of the other boys but not all of them, running in the middle of the pack. Not bad, she thought. Not terrible. And then she was running side by side with Benji True, who had crossed over two lanes to join her.

"Go on," she said. "I'm molasses on the track."

"No problem," Benji said. "I'm not fast."

"Right," Julie said. "I can tell you're very slow."

If it was a contest, which the coach said it was not, Benji and Julie came in fourth, neck and neck, crossing the finish line just after Andy Dunn, a yard or so behind Blue Kantor and Stan Fish.

"He's not so bad, Julie," Lila said later. "He's trying to be friends."

"So?"

"So give him a chance," Lila said.

The coach tried Benji in goal first, and as it turned out, he was very good.

"Amazing," the coach said. "You must have put in some time at goal, Ben."

"Four years," Benji said. "I played for two teams in Darien."

"Not bad," the coach said. He looked up at Julie.

"You're trying goal, Julie?"

"I think," Julie said.

"You ought to try defense," the coach said in private when Julie came down from the bench to the field. "There's going to be a lot of competition for goal."

She shrugged.

"I'm trying for goalie," she said.

It wasn't fair. She had worked all summer, all year when the weather was good, practicing and practicing.

And Benji True was going to be the goalie. He wasn't even from Newtown. He didn't belong here. He hadn't spent years playing with the boys on the Bucks County team like she had. He didn't deserve it.

Besides, he was ruining her life.

"Julie MacNeil?" the coach called.

It was her turn.

Terry Winner had tried out already, and he was better than she remembered, but not great. Not good enough to beat Benji True for the position, and probably not good enough to stop the Doylestown or New Hope team.

"Watch out for Tom Baer," the coach said as she suited up in her pads and goalie mask. "He has a tricky kick, and so does Tucker."

Tom Baer had always been the high scorer, ever since Julie began to play. But she had never played on the same team with Tucker Ryan and wasn't prepared for his speed, how hard he kicked, straight at her, into her belly, knocking her over backward, knocking the wind out of her, the fast ball slipping by her into the goal.

Tom Baer kicked the second goal. She could see that he was going to kick the ball without passing, running straight down the field, and she was prepared, leaning forward, her arms out, certain she could catch the ball, which came right toward her.

But the ball had such a fierce spin that she dropped it the minute it was in her hands.

She caught the third kick at goal from Timo Rivers, a lazy kicker, but fast. She had to run for it because it came at an angle toward the goal, and then she slid into the ball, falling on her stomach, but she stopped it, and she could hear scattered cheering from the bench where Lila sat with Benji True. It was not a great catch, but it was good, she told herself.

She was in the game for ten of the longest minutes she could ever remember when the coach called for Tucker Ryan to try at goal.

"Not bad," the coach said as Julie walked off the field.

"Terrible," Julie said.

And then, to her surprise and sadness, Tucker Ryan stopped every ball that came his way but one.

"You were great, Jules," Lila said, walking back to the locker room. But Julie shook her head.

"Not good enough," she said.

"Not as good as Benji, maybe," Lila said. "But good. Honestly, Julie, I think you'll make the team."

"Not a chance," Julie said.

"Second team," Lila said. "Back-up goalie."

"Tucker Ryan will be back-up goalie. And then Terry

Winner," Julie said. "Coach Harrison isn't going to have a girl on his team, and that's that."

They walked through the swinging doors and down the corridor to their lockers, sitting down on the bench together. Julie took off her shorts and T-shirt and sneakers, stuffed them into her locker, and put her school clothes on.

"I don't even know if I want to play on a team with that creep," she said, slinging her book bag over her shoulder.

"He's nice to you, though," Lila said. "Nicer than most boys, you have to admit."

He was nice to her. Or else he was playing up to her, trying to be friends because his mother told him he had to, told him that because of Jack MacNeil, Benji must pull himself together and act like the sort of boy Jack MacNeil would want to have around.

Just the thought made Julie's stomach weak.

"The coach said the team is going to be posted in a minute," Lila asked. "Do you want to wait to see it?"

"Nope," Julie said. "I have to pick up Tally at the library and then go to the drugstore and then home."

"I'll come with you to the drugstore too," Lila said.

"I thought Beatrice was coming over to play at your barn," Julie said with a twinge of sadness.

"Later, after her piano lesson," Lila said. "You can come if you like." She shrugged. "But I'm sure you're too busy."

"Probably," Julie said.

* * *

When Julie arrived at New's Drugstore, Benji True was standing in the aisle looking at comic books. She tried to slip unseen into the candy aisle.

"It's too late," Lila said. "He's seen you."

"Great," Julie said

Benji came up behind them. "Hiya," he said. "What are you guys doing?"

"Not much," Julie said. "Tally has a dentist appointment."

"No, I don't," Tally said. "I just had a dentist appointment."

"Wrong," Julie said. "I got a note from Daddy that you do have a dentist appointment."

"I have a friend coming over," Lila said.

"I was looking for something to do until my mother gets home from work," Benji said. "I don't have a lot of friends here yet."

"You will soon," Tally said.

Julie took a package of peanut M&M's.

"I guess you saw the list of the soccer team on the bulletin board," Benji said, following her to the cash register.

"I bet you made first-string goalie," Julie said.

"And you made alternate goalie," Benji said.

Julie's heart skipped a beat.

"Nope," she said.

"Well, you did," Benji said. "You'll be the only girl on our team."

"I thought Tucker or Terry was going to be alternate goalie."

"Terry didn't make the team, and Tucker's a halfback," Benji said.

"Well," Julie said, "we're probably moving to Philadelphia on Saturday."

And she walked out of the drugstore, holding Tally's hand, leaving Lila to talk to the creep, Benji True.

"See you," she called. "We have to go home."

"Are we going home for real now?" Tally asked quietly.

"For real," Julie said.

Julie never liked the first moment of arriving home after school. In her absence, the house had grown chilly and damp; the smell of breakfast lingering in the hall, a loneliness about the empty rooms, a sense of something missing.

And this afternoon, she wasn't prepared for the sight of Alicia MacNeil all over the walls of the living room and dining room and kitchen—her mother's face bathed in light, her eyes lively against her dark skin.

She went into the kitchen and sank down at the table, weak with sadness.

"What's for snack?" Tally asked, looking into the empty cookie jar. "Daddy finished the chocolate chips."

"Maybe apples," Julie said, not at all hungry herself.

"Don't we have something yummier than apples?" Tally asked.

"Apples are good for you," Julie said automatically.

She watched her sister searching through the refrigerator.

"Can I make cinnamon toast?" Tally asked, taking a loaf of bread out of the fridge.

"Not too much sugar."

Tally poured sugar and cinnamon on a piece of bread.

"Want one?" she asked.

Julie shook her head.

"You seem weird," Tally said, turning on the toaster oven, slipping the bread under the burner.

"I'm fine," Julie said. "But be careful the toast doesn't burn."

"Why do you seem so weird?" Tally asked, sitting down beside her sister. "Is it because of goalie tryouts?"

"I don't even care about goalie tryouts," Julie said. "I was actually just wondering if you ever miss our mother."

"I guess," Tally said. "Sometimes when my friends talk about 'Mommy' and I can't think of our mother as Mommy because I never even saw her. Then I feel left out." She checked the cinnamon toast, taking it out of the oven.

"Get a plate, Tal," Julie said. "Don't just eat on the table."

"Anyway, I can't miss her too much because I have you all the time taking her place." She sat upright, lowered her voice, and imitated Julie's voice. "'Get a plate, Tal,'" she said. "'Be careful of the toaster oven. Not too much sugar, Tally. Apples are good for you.'"

"I don't want to be bossy," Julie said quietly. "Sometimes I simply want a regular life without responsibility for you and Monk and Ernestine and dinner and the laundry. Sometimes," she said, turning her face away so Tally couldn't see the tears struggling to the surface of her eyes, "I wish our mother was here to take care of everything, and then I get mad at her for getting killed."

Tally looked up, surprised. "But it wasn't her fault, was it?"

Julie shook her head. "It wasn't her fault, but I can't help being mad. It just happens," she said, "and it's hard to just be mad. You feel like being mad at someone."

"Well, you seem to be pretty mad at Eliza True," Tally said.

"I am," Julie said fiercely.

"She's not the worst person I've ever met," Tally said.

"Not unless she marries our father," Julie said.

"Marries our father?" Tally asked. "Why do you think she's going to marry our father?"

"Because of what Lila said to us," Julie said.

Tally sat very quietly in the chair, picking at the cinnamon toast, giving small bites to an agreeable Ernestine sitting on the kitchen table between them.

"You really think it's true?" Tally asked.

"I don't know." Julie shrugged. "Ask Daddy."

Tally dumped the rest of her snack on the floor for Monk.

"I think we should move to Aunt Melinda's," Julie said.

* * *

58

Aunt Melinda said no, not immediately, not until Sunday because she had guests coming on Saturday. "What is suddenly making you unhappy?" Aunt Melinda asked.

"I'm not so unhappy," Julie said.

But she was unhappy, near tears, heartsick, her stomach a dark empty well inside her.

"Something more happened," Melinda said.

"You probably already know," Julie said. "Daddy has probably told the whole world, leaving us for last."

"Your father hasn't told me anything, Jules," Aunt Melinda said.

"I don't like the woman who came for dinner last night," Julie said. "I think she wants to make Daddy marry her."

"No one can *make* your father do anything, sweet pea," Aunt Melinda said. "He's taken wonderful care of two little girls all by himself for a long time."

"Right," Julie began, "but doesn't it upset you that Daddy is going to replace our mother with someone else?"

There was a long silence. Julie could hear Melinda's soft breathing.

"We don't know that's what's going on, Jules," Aunt Melinda said.

"But if something is going on," Julie began, "then are you upset?"

"I'd be sad if your father married again, but not for him and not for you. I'd be sad because my sister died too young to see her darling children."

59

"That's what I mean," Julie said. "That's why we have to stop it from happening."

"But Julie," Melinda said. "I can't change the way things are. I can't stop time from rolling on or stop you from growing up or stop your father from making a life for himself because he lost the life he loved."

"Yes, you can," Julie said, and she was weeping.

"I wouldn't want to stop him or you or Tally or any of us from making new lives without your mother. Because we can't change the fact that she isn't here."

"I was hoping you'd be helpful," Julie said. And she hung up the telephone.

Melinda didn't call back immediately, but she called back soon, and Julie let the phone ring, listening to her message on the answering machine: "This is Melinda for Julie to say I'm always here, on the second floor of eight sixteen Locust Street or in the third-grade classroom of Germantown Friends, ready to come get you in a flash if you need me." Her voice was warm and cheerful, and although Julie didn't pick up the phone or call her back, just the sound of Melinda's voice made her feel better.

Julie didn't cook dinner. Her father called at five to say he'd be an hour or so late for dinner, and what was she thinking of cooking.

"Cereal," Julie said.

"Just cereal?" her father asked.

"Why should I cook anything else when you're never

home and Tally and me are perfectly happy with just cereal with vanilla ice cream on top, maybe," she said.

She didn't hang up exactly, but she didn't say good-bye.

"I liked it better when we had real dinners and you cooked mashed potatoes and things," Tally said while Julie was reading to her from *Charlotte's Web.*

"Me too," Julie said. "But tonight I'm too mad at Daddy to cook. I want him to eat cereal and go to bed hungry."

"Me too," Tally said loyally, listening as Julie read the sad end of Charlotte's precious spider life.

"Julie?" she began when Julie had finished reading.

"Yes?"

"Maybe you should be the best, the best cook, the best cleaner, the best mother, the best everything in the world so Daddy won't need to have a girlfriend."

"That's what I do, Tal," Julie said.

"But maybe when he comes home for dinner you should make roast beef and chocolate cake instead of cereal."

Julie shook her head.

"He only deserves cereal," she said.

She was doing her math homework with Monk under her desk when her father drove up in his car. She heard him open the front door and call to her, but she didn't answer.

She heard Tally calling, "Hi, Daddy," heard her run down the steps full of high spirits, but Julie continued to work on fractions.

Her father didn't come upstairs right away. Julie kept checking her watch. He had been home for more than fifteen minutes before she heard his footsteps on the stairs, heard him knock on her bedroom door and open it.

"Hiya, chum," he said cheerfully. "The cereal was first rate. Tally tells me it's granola from now on." He crossed the room and kissed the top of her head. "So are we going to have a conversation?"

"I don't think so," Julie said. "I have a lot of homework to do tonight."

"Well, if you change your mind," he said. "I'm in my room writing my program for tomorrow."

"Melinda called," Julie said. "She's very upset."

"About what?" her father asked.

"She's upset about our mother," Julie said.

"Then we better talk about things, chum," her father said.

"I don't have time to talk about things," Julie said. "If you want to find out why she's upset, call her."

It was nine o'clock when Julie finished her homework, got into her pajamas, brushed her teeth, let Monk out in the backyard to pee, and came upstairs, Monk bounding behind her with his yellow tennis ball. The door to her father's room was closed and she stopped beside it, considering. She put her ear next to the door and listened, hearing voices. He seemed to be talking on the telephone. She heard the muffled sound of his voice.

When she went in, he was on the phone, but she could tell he wasn't talking to Melinda. He put his hand over the receiver.

"Good night," she said.

"Just a sec, chum," he said. "I'll be right off."

"Never mind," Julie said. "I only wanted to say good night."

And she shut the door to his bedroom, went into her room with Monk, and locked her door.

When her father knocked and tried the door, she didn't answer.

"Julie," he said firmly, "I don't want your door locked."

"Too bad," she said. "It's locked already, and I'm asleep."

Julie couldn't sleep. She lay on top of her covers, Monk's large head on her belly, and looked out the window at the scattering of stars over the river. The clock beside her bed said eleven o'clock, but she was wide awake, too anxious to sleep.

The house was almost silent, Tally sleeping on her stomach with Ernestine curled around the top of her head, her father's light out. But she thought she could hear the sound of conversation. She tiptoed down the hall and stopped at her father's room. At first she could hear nothing at all, although she had a sense that he was awake. And then she heard his muffled voice. She leaned against the door and listened to the sound of his voice. He must be talking on the telephone. She had never known him to actually talk on the telephone. His conversations were always swift and businesslike, even with Julie when he was at work.

At first she thought of going in, opening the door without knocking, standing in the darkness just inside his room.

Who're you talking to in the middle of the night, she could say. *You're keeping me awake.* Although she was sure she knew who he was talking to. She could feel Eliza True on the other end of the phone.

Please hang up, she could say. *I need to talk with you.*

She tiptoed past his door and down the steps into the kitchen, where she found some old oatmeal cookies. She stuffed them into her pocket and went into the living room. She turned on a small light next to the sofa and sank into the soft pillows, patting the cushion for Monk to hop up. The room seemed strangely unfamiliar in the muted light, and before she even remembered that the dark walls were plastered with pictures of her mother, she felt self-conscious, as though she were the subject of someone's secret examination.

She turned on another light, enough light to see the pictures, although the room was still too dark to identify the faces of her mother specifically.

She wondered, did her mother know that Julie had filled the house with her pictures, did she feel suddenly released from the boxes of photographs where she had been trapped?

She climbed over Monk and opened the doors at the bottom of the bookcase where the photograph albums were kept, opening and shutting one after another until she came to the older ones of her mother at ten or eleven, Julie's age, a tall, thin, narrow-faced blond girl. *Me as a Girl Scout. Me as a fifth-grader in Mrs. Harrow's class—Yuk! Me as a pirate on Halloween. Me with Maman at the zoo. Me and Melinda at Lake of the Woods Summer Camp.* But most of the pictures, pages and pages of them, were of her mother in uniforms. *Me playing soccer with the Wolves' A Team. Me playing ice hockey with Tommy Rocket. Me playing tennis on the Bryn Mawr campus and losing. Me playing in the twelve and under tournament and winning a blue ribbon. Me as captain of the soccer team.*

The girl in the pictures was familiar to Julie—not exactly familiar, but enough like Julie in the way she stood, the way she turned her head just slightly to the side, the shy half-smile, the fierce bright eyes, for Julie to feel kinship.

She put the albums away. Monk was sleeping on the couch, filling it up, his head on the pillow. Julie slid over him, wedging herself into the tiny space he had left in the corner, and sometime between a moment of looking at the wall of pictures behind her and morning, she fell asleep.

When she woke up, the living room was bright with the beginning of a sunny day, and her father was standing beside the couch. He might have been standing there for a long time—she had a sense of him in her sleep, but when she opened her eyes he was there in a robe, his arms folded across his chest, and he had his glasses on.

"What's up, chum?" he asked.

She had never noticed before the way his hair was speckled with gray, and he wasn't even forty yet. She worried about him sometimes, worried that he looked older than other fathers his age, older than Lila's father.

"It must be difficult for your amazing father raising two girls alone," Lila's mother had said to Julie that summer. It occurred to Julie, noticing the way his skin hung in little pockets underneath his eyes, that maybe it was too difficult for her father to be alone in spite of everything she did to help.

"Couldn't sleep?" he asked.

Julie stretched.

"Nope," she said. "I heard you talking on the phone, and it kept me awake."

She didn't mean to say anything, not first thing in the morning before she had a chance to think about it, but she couldn't help herself.

He sat down on the couch beside her.

"I'm sorry I was keeping you awake," he said.

"Were you talking to Melinda?" Julie asked, knowing the answer, of course, expecting somehow that he would say, *Yes, I was talking to Melinda,* even though it wasn't true. But he did not. He put his feet up on the coffee table, leaned back against the couch, and told her he had been talking to Eliza True.

"Is she your girlfriend?" Julie asked, her heart in her mouth, not wishing to hear the news.

"I like her," he said.

"So," Julie said, sitting up behind Monk, keeping him between her and her father, "I suppose you don't need me any longer."

"It's not a question of needing you, chum," Jack MacNeil said quietly. "I don't think of it as needing you. You are my daughter. You were my daughter long before I met Eliza."

In the kitchen, Julie made herself a bowl of cereal and sat down at the table with Ernestine, watching her father make coffee.

She was not going to make coffee for him again, she thought, or pancakes, or poached eggs, his favorite, or cut up strawberries for his cereal. She would take care of Tally and Monk and Ernestine, and that was all.

"I don't think you should give Eliza True my mother's wedding ring," she said finally, twisting the gold band on her thumb.

"I wouldn't dream of it," her father said. "It's the ring I gave to your mother."

"Well, it's mine now," Julie said matter-of-factly.

Tally fell in love with Eliza True.

"I don't know what to do about it," Julie said on the telephone to her aunt Melinda in October.

"It's probably nice for Tally, sweet pea," Melinda said. "She's never had a mother."

"Well, it's not nice for me," Julie said. "And I can't do anything about it except move in with you."

Melinda said she would love to have Julie move in with her, that she was welcome in Philadelphia anytime for days or weeks or months.

"But there is something you can do about it, Jules," she said.

"Like what?" Julie asked glumly.

"Like playing soccer and going for sleep overs with your

friends and to birthday parties, all the things you haven't done because you've had so much responsibility."

"I liked the responsibility."

"Well, according to your father, you still have plenty of it."

"Hardly any," Julie said sadly. "It's as if I don't even need to live here any longer. It's not my home."

The night before, Eliza True had cooked dinner; chicken and vegetables with fruit for dessert. No ice cream, no cereal, no pancakes. She had even stayed to read Tally *Abel's Island* while Benji did his homework at the dining-room table and Julie sulked in her room with Monk.

"Are they going to move in with us?" Julie had asked her father when he came in to kiss her good night.

"Of course not, chum," her father had said. "We're just becoming friends."

But Julie didn't believe him.

She couldn't get to sleep at night for thinking.

She thought of how the house would be when Eliza True and Benji moved in. She'd have to move into the room with Tally and give up her room to Benji, which was the best room, with built-in bookcases and a window seat overlooking the garden. She'd be stuffed in Tally's room without a desk or room for a chair or a bookcase. She'd have to do her homework downstairs with Benji, the creep, sitting at the dining-room table. And worst of all, Eliza True would move into the room with her father. She tried to think of how that would be and couldn't.

* * *

"I went to Lila O'Shee's birthday party last Sunday," Julie said defensively to Melinda. "And I am playing soccer, but only during practice. I don't get to do anything except sit on the bench during games, so what kind of fun is that?"

There had been six games already, every Saturday at two on the high-school field, and so far Newtown had a 6–0 record while Julie sat on the bench in her uniform, waiting for her chance.

"Soon, Julie," Coach Harrison said. "Maybe next game."

But so far the scores had been too close to take a chance on Julie. At least that's what Tommy Tyler and Tucker Ryan had told her.

"You're good MacNeil," they said. "Just not as good as Benji."

It was late October, when the days were getting shorter and colder and a feeling of sadness was in the air, matching exactly the sadness Julie had felt since her life had turned on her.

Everything on which she had counted, her father, her sister, her role in the family, even dependable Aunt Melinda, had changed.

"You'll get your chance to play, chum," her father said to her one rare evening at dinner when Eliza True was not there and they got to have mashed potatoes and ice cream like they used to. "You won't be on the bench forever."

"So what?" Julie shrugged. "I'm on the bench everywhere in my life," she said.

Which was how it felt.

She had been replaced, put out to pasture like an old horse, no longer a player at home, no longer needed, not Tally's mother or her father's helpmate, just his older daughter, Julie MacNeil.

And that wasn't good enough.

On the night of her father's birthday in late October, there was a family birthday party with Aunt Melinda, who came up from Philadelphia, and Eliza True and Benji and Aunt Melinda's boyfriend. At the end of it, Julie lost her temper.

The tantrum had been coming for a long time, but when it happened, when she exploded at the dining-room table just before the birthday cake, she surprised even herself.

Dinner, which Eliza True had cooked with Melinda's help, was in the dining room with candles on the table and everyone chattering cheerfully, except Julie, who didn't speak unless someone spoke to her. She picked at her dinner, separating the vegetables from the roast beef, hiding the beets under the mashed potatoes, hanging her head over her plate, thinking of disappearing.

Would anyone mind or care at all if she disappeared, she asked herself, especially her father, now happy as summer to have Eliza True around to help. Maybe he'd even be glad to have Julie out of his way now, she'd turned so difficult.

Melinda was in the kitchen putting the candles on the birthday cake.

"Want to help, Jules?" she'd asked when she got up from the table.

Julie shook her head.

Benji was clearing the table, and Julie was sitting with her chin in her fists, a small volcano heating away inside her ready to erupt.

And then, out of the blue, without even an invitation, Tally, whom Julie had taken care of every single day of her life since their mother was killed, got up from the table, skipped around to the seat where Eliza True was sitting, and climbed onto her lap.

There was a white tablecloth on the table, water and wine glasses, and some silverware, although most of the plates had been cleared by Benji. Julie leapt up, grabbed the corner of the tablecloth, and pulled it with all her might, scattering the glasses, spilling water and juice and milk and wine all over the table, over Eliza True and Tally and her father, the silverware flying, the remaining plates crashing to the ground.

"I hate you all," she cried, running through the house and out the front door, down the lane to the river, running as fast as she could run in the near-black darkness, hearing Monk bounding after her. At the towpath, silver lit from a full moon, Monk at her heels, Julie walked north in the direction of New Hope, tears chilly on her cheeks, her anger dissipating in the autumn air.

She would not go back, she told herself. She would walk with Monk to the end of the river and disappear.

* * *

The river was eerie at night, black water splashing against the rocks and shore; the sound of life, of animals or people or worse; Monk skittish beside her, sensing danger. If she stopped, she wouldn't be able to hear if anyone was following, because of the rush of water and the wind in the trees.

Someone should come, she thought to herself. Her father. Or Tally. Or Aunt Melinda. Soon.

When she came to a log crossing the path in front of her, she sat down on it. Monk stood beside her, his ears lifted above the crown of his head, the hair bristly on the back of his neck, alert. That much she could see in the moonlight. What she couldn't see was down the long dark path from which she had come or ahead of her—a sea of blackness with just a sprinkle of moonlight like sugar on the tops of the trees.

The log was damp on her jeans, the air cold, and she didn't have a sweater. Somewhere on the towpath in the direction of her own house, she began to hear a rustling, more like whispering than the actual sound of footsteps, and she thought she saw light, but it could have been light dropped to earth from the moon. She sat very still, waiting, counting on Monk in case of trouble.

Monk's growling started very deep in his stomach, his mouth closed, a *grrr* like hunger rolling inside him, and the sound was sufficient to muffle the sound Julie had been hearing on the path, but she could see there was a light, too isolated to be moonlight. A figure, an apparition in the distance, a shadow of human shape was calling something Julie couldn't hear, because Monk was standing now, barking with a ferocity she had never heard from him before, sharp fierce barks, punctuated by a growl. She could imagine his lips had curled back, exposing his long and competent teeth.

"Julie!" She was sure she heard someone call her name. "Julie!"

But Monk was making too much noise to hear.

"Yes," she shouted above the barking. She guessed it was her father.

"Who is it?" she called again, taking hold of Monk's collar, patting his head to calm the barking.

"Benji."

She couldn't believe it. Benji True instead of her father. Or Aunt Melinda or Tally. Certainly she would never speak to them again.

She sat very still.

"Where are you?" Benji called. "I can't see you."

Monk had calmed down, no longer barking, a low growl rumbling in his belly, but he had sat down next to Julie, his ears still up and the hair on his back settled.

"I'm here," Julie said, and she watched him walk toward her like a black ghost, preceded by a yellow circle skittering across the ground from the flashlight he carried.

"I expected my father," she said coolly.

"I said I wanted to come," Benji said, reaching the place where Julie was sitting, patting Monk on the head. "It's really scary back here, isn't it."

"Not so scary to me," Julie said.

He sat down next to her on the log.

"So I guess I ruined the birthday," Julie said.

"They're waiting for you to come back," Benji said.

"They can wait until next year," Julie said. "I'm not coming back."

"I know," Benji said quietly.

"How do you know?" Julie asked crossly.

"I mean I know how you feel," Benji said. "That's all. That's why I came out here. Your father ran after you, and so did Tally." He moved over a little closer to Julie, and she could feel him shivering. "But I said I wanted to come because I knew how you felt and they didn't."

"You can't know exactly because your mother isn't dead," Julie said.

"No," Benji said. "But my father is gone, and my mother wants to make a new family with your family. And I don't," he said. "I want the family I used to have with my own father in Connecticut in the house where I grew up where I used to have a dog like Monk called Mercy and we had to give him away when my parents got divorced."

Julie sat very still. They sat together for a long time without talking, the moon spreading silver light across their hands and legs spread out in front of them, across Monk's black coat of hair. In the distance, they could hear the voices of Eliza True and Jack MacNeil, the high and anxious cry of Tally's voice. But for what seemed to be a long time, they didn't answer to the calling.

"I guess at least we better go back to your father's birthday," Benji said finally.

"I guess we should," Julie said, and they followed the light circle dancing down the path in front of them home.

The day of the championship soccer game was glorious, mid-November, heavy-sweater weather, cold but bright and sunny, the air like clear spring water.

Julie woke up sick.

"I think you're nervous," her father said, sitting at the end of the bed.

"Whatever," Julie replied.

Her stomach fluttered like birds inside of her, and she felt shaky all over. "But there's nothing for me to be nervous about. I never play."

"Come down and have a little tea and toast, chum," her father said, patting the top of her head. "See if that makes you feel better."

Tally sat at the end of the bed, holding an unhappy Ernestine, who did not wish to be held.

"We were going to have a picnic with the Trues," Tally said sadly.

"Break my heart," Julie said, climbing out of bed.

The Trues had improved in the last weeks. She did like Benji a little better since her father's birthday. In fact, if his mother didn't want to be the new mother of the MacNeil family, she might have liked Benji True very much. They might have been friends, even the best of friends. But as it was, they were friendly but not at all the best of friends.

Downstairs she slid into the chair beside her father and sipped the hot tea, resting her bare feet on Monk's back.

"It's not that I'm nervous," she said to her father. "It's something else."

For many nights, before she went to sleep she had imagined this Saturday in November, the final game, the championships. Mostly, she imagined everyone in the bleachers around the soccer field, her little family and Eliza True and Lila and the O'Shees and all of her friends at school and all of her teachers. She was on the bench while Benjamin True, new boy from Connecticut, was the hero, saving every goal, holding the opposing team to a score of zero, leading the team to the county soccer championship and a trophy and free lunch at Cindy's Takeout.

Occasionally she imagined herself as the one in the goal, holding the other team to a score of zero, stopping spin balls kicked straight at her stomach, flying in the air to stop a corner kick, falling on ground balls. But she never was really able to think how she could have gotten there in place of Benji True.

When the telephone rang, it was Benji for Julie.

Julie shook her head. "I don't want to talk."

"'Cause she's sick," Tally said crossly, as if Julie had chosen on purpose to be sick in order to cancel the picnic with the Trues.

"Should I tell him you don't feel well?" her father asked.

"Don't tell him anything," Julie said.

Her father went back to the telephone.

"He wants to talk to you for just a second," he said holding his hand over the receiver so Benji couldn't hear what he was saying. "He says *he* feels sick."

"Great." Julie took over the telephone. "Just what the team needs for the championship."

He didn't know whether he was really sick or just nervous, he told her, but he had been up all night, and now he didn't feel like eating breakfast, and nothing like this had ever happened before a game in all the years he lived in Connecticut.

"Are you okay?" he asked.

"I'm fine," Julie said to him. "But I don't have anything to be nervous about."

"I thought you felt sick," Tally said when Julie hung up.

"I do, dumbbell," Julie said. "But it's none of Benji True's business."

She finished her tea, ate a little of her toast, and got up to dress for the game.

"So you are playing?" Tally asked. "We're going to get to have a picnic?"

"No, I'm not playing, Tally," Julie said. "I'm getting dressed."

"In your soccer clothes?" Tally asked.

"Exactly," Julie said, motioning for Monk to follow her upstairs.

"I think Julie's crazy," Tally said as Julie left the room.

"Worried," her father said.

"Not worried or crazy," Julie called from the stairs. "Nobody in this family knows a thing about me except Monk."

Upstairs, she got her soccer uniform, number thirty-three, out of the closet and dressed. The uniform was sparkling new. It had never been washed, had never had a chance to get dirty. She dressed quickly, brushed her hair into a high ponytail, and put on her baseball cap bill backward so, without hair showing, she could pass for a boy. She did that for every game.

"Feel a little better?" her father asked, coming upstairs.

"Nope," Julie said.

"Well, you will," he said. "As soon as things get started." He patted her head.

Julie took her mother's wedding ring out of the top

drawer, where she kept it on game days so she wouldn't lose it in case she played.

She slipped the ring on her thumb.

"Are you sure you want to wear that to the game?" her father asked. "It might get lost."

"I'm sure," Julie said. "For good luck. Just in case. I'll be careful."

The MacNeils were late. Tally lost her shoe and kept changing outfits, and then Ernestine brought another mouse in from the garden which had to be gotten rid of, and the car wouldn't start. So by the time they arrived at the soccer field behind the high school, it was one-fifteen and almost everyone from both teams was already there practicing on the field.

In the distance, standing alone, Julie could see Eliza True. She was in blue jeans and a heavy sweater, her arms folded across her chest, and somehow, seeing her there separated from the crowd made her seem less dangerous to Julie.

In the MacNeil house, where she came for dinner two or three times a week and always on Saturday, playing with Tally, hiking with Monk and her father along the river, sometimes cooking, always washing up, filling the house with conversation, Eliza seemed dangerous, as if the MacNeils' lives together as a family would never be the same again. The small things she did were the worst. She organized the silverware drawer neatly every week, and every week when she wasn't there, Julie spilled the silver from the dishwasher all together, the knives and forks and spoons all mixed up. She put the sugar in the cupboard, and Julie took it out and put it on the kitchen table. She rearranged the fridge in sections. And she played classical music on the radio.

"Listen," she'd say. "Isn't that a Beethoven sonata, Jack?"

It drove Julie crazy. Her father had never mentioned Beethoven before.

"We don't know about sonatas and stuff," Julie said to her once. "We don't listen to that kind of music unless you're around."

Later that night, her father told her that part of friendship is learning from other people, and the MacNeils were learning about music from Eliza.

"Yuk," Julie said.

But lately Julie was getting used to Eliza. She wasn't exactly liking her better, but she was noticing her less when she was around. Sometimes she even forgot the classical music was playing. In fact the week before the championships, they had been sitting around the kitchen table with pizzas, when Benji had said, "Isn't that a Beethoven sonata, Julie?" and everyone had laughed, even Eliza.

Julie still wouldn't talk to her in a personal way. Eliza tried. She tried safe subjects with Julie like school and sports and her grandmother's summer cottage in the Adirondacks.

She tried Christmas and Thanksgiving, asking what kinds of celebrations the MacNeil family had for these holidays. Sometimes she even tried to talk about friendship or fears or worries, and once she brought up Julie's mother.

"I don't talk about her to anyone but Daddy," Julie said coolly.

And Eliza apologized for bringing her up.

That night her father asked about the pictures. The downstairs was still full of the pictures of Alicia MacNeil plastered on the walls. When occasionally the tape holding them lost its stickiness and one or two fell off, Julie would put new tape on the back and stick it up again.

"Listen chum, I've been thinking about the pictures," her father said when he came in to kiss her good night.

"What about them?"

"Well, I've been thinking we need a few pictures in frames of your mother, but not so many," he said. "What do you think?"

Julie had looked at him without affection. "I think we need them all," she said. "That's why Tally and I put them up."

But sometimes lately, Julie was even sorry when Eliza and Benji got back in their blue Toyota to drive home. Afterward the MacNeil house suddenly seemed a little empty without them.

"My mother said you might not come," Benji said, putting on his mask, walking with Julie over to the hill where the coach had assembled the team for a pep talk.

84

"Well, I'm here," Julie said sarcastically. "Ready to save the game for Newtown in case you get sick."

"You might need to," Benji said.

"Fat chance," Julie said.

Doylestown had been the champions for four years running. This year the team was bigger than Newtown, taller and larger, with a reputation for speed and aggression. They had two first stringers on the all-county team from the year before, one terrific girl, Holly Acton, known all over as Speedo, who played center, and the best goalie of any team, including Benji True.

"Do you think you have a chance?" Eliza True asked, coming up behind Julie, who had taken her place on the bench as the teams gathered on the field for the kickoff.

"A little but not much," Julie said. "Number thirty-six and number forty-one on the Doylestown team are amazing, and so is the goalie."

"That's what Benji told me," she said. "He has a creepy feeling about today, he says."

"He told me he feels sick," Julie said.

"Nervous," Eliza said. "Good luck," she said to Julie. "Good luck, guys," she said to the rest of the team.

Doylestown made the first goal in the second minute of the first quarter, a direct hit at the goal that took Benji completely by surprise. Benji threw his arms up in the air in an expression of anger at himself for missing the ball, and

Coach Harrison called a time-out, gathering the team in the middle of the field for a quick pep talk.

"Keep your heads," he said gruffly. "This team is aggressive, and you're going to have to be quick and alert. Play an offensive game. Keep the ball at their end of the field, and shoot at the goal."

"Brother," Benji whispered to Julie. "I was afraid of this."

"Never mind," Julie said. "It just got started so fast. You'll do okay." And to her surprise, she hugged him without thinking.

In the rest of the first quarter, Newtown and Doylestown were evenly matched, both playing well without a score. Trevor Mann on the Newtown team sprained his ankle, and the center of Doylestown had the wind knocked out of her and had to sit out the rest of the quarter.

"This is a rough game," Richie Olds, sitting on the bench next to Julie, said. "I'm glad I'm not in it."

"Me too," Julie said.

And in fact, she was very glad. There was too much nervous tension in the air. For the first time that season, she was happy that it was Benji True in the goal and not her. She didn't want the responsibility for losing.

The second quarter began slowly with three fouls called early, two against Doylestown. And then, less than two minutes into the quarter, number forty-one got the ball, taking it straight from center down the field alone with a kick to the goal which Benji missed. The Doylestown stands went wild, and Julie noticed Benji flop facedown in the goal as if the wind had been knocked out of him too.

"Do you think he's okay?" Julie asked Richie.

"I think he's mad," Richie said. "He hasn't let a goal get through since he came to Newtown."

But Benji got up very slowly and leaned against the side of the goal and seemed to Julie less mad than hurt.

Eliza True must have noticed the same thing, because she came over to ask the coach if Benji had been hurt, and the coach said no, Benji was fine, just upset. The game, with a score of 2–0 Doylestown, started again with Ted Brandon at center for Newtown. The first kick was deep into the opposing team's territory, but Newtown couldn't score. Each time the ball got close to the opposing goal, the Doylestown defense took possession.

By halftime, Benji was exhausted. He had stopped another goal just before halftime, but when the whistle blew for the end of the second quarter, he dragged himself to the side of the field and flopped down on his back.

"Are you okay?" Coach Harrison asked him.

"Okay enough," Benji said, waving away his mother who had come to check on him. "I'm tired," he said, sitting up to eat an orange. "Sorry about the scores, Coach, but Doylestown is amazing."

"They're good," the coach said. "But you guys can win if the offense gets it together," he said to the team gathered around him at the bench. "Be aggressive."

Just before the second half began, Benji looked pale and

unhappy, and the coach knelt down to ask him if he was okay to play.

"Fine," Benji said.

"You better be okay," Julie said. "I sure don't want to play against this team. They'll kill me."

Benji shrugged. "They're pretty tough," he said.

The third quarter was slow. Both teams seemed overtired, missing passes, fouling, kicking outside the goal, making mistake after mistake. Newtown made one goal toward the end of the quarter, an easy goal, but even then the excitement didn't begin to build until the end of the quarter when, with two minutes to go, number forty-one stole the ball from Newtown and took it three quarters down the field at a tear, no one at all in his way. When the low hard kick came toward the goal, Benji stopped it, but after the whistle blew for a time-out, Benji True was lying on his back on the ground, his arms stretched out on either side of him.

Julie leapt up from the bench, Coach Harrison and the Doylestown coach beside her, running all the way down the field to the goal where Benji lay absolutely still. She was there first, down on her knees beside him.

"Are you okay?" she asked, although it was a crazy question since he certainly wasn't okay at all, his eyes open, his face squinched up in pain.

He shook his head.

The coach knelt down, and Dr. Vance was right behind him.

"My knee kills," Benji said.

The doctor checked his arms, his legs, his knees.

"I think you've twisted the cartilage, Benji." He stood back. "Can you move it?"

Benji tried, but the leg wasn't cooperating.

"I don't think so," he said. "It feels on fire."

"Do you need a stretcher?" the doctor asked.

"I can hop," Benji said.

So Julie and Tom Baer got on either side of him and helped him to his feet, but as he had thought, he couldn't put any weight on the leg, so he hopped over to the bench, his arms slung around their necks.

"So," Coach Harrison said to the referee and the coach of the Doylestown team. "What do you think?"

"We're ready to begin again whenever you are," the Doylestown coach said. "Do you have a sub for goalie?"

Julie's stomach fell. She leaned against Benji.

"MacNeil?" Coach Harrison said. "Ready?"

"Ready," Julie said.

But she wasn't ready at all.

She put on the face mask which Benji had taken off and given her, and the shin pads which the coach had taken off Benji's legs so he could ice his knee, and leaned down to double-knot her cleats.

"Good luck," Benji said, reaching into his pocket for something, handing it to her as she left. "It's for good luck," he said. "I always carry it."

She didn't even take time to look at what he had given her, stuffing it into the pocket of her shorts, running down the field toward the goal with her teammates cheering.

"The goalie is a girl," she heard shouted from far across the field where the Doylestown team was in position to begin again, and along the sidelines, just above the goal, she saw her father standing with Tally, Tally cheering, "Go Julie," just before the whistle blew to begin.

There was something about a girl in the goal, or Benji getting hurt, or the substitute goalie playing, which fired up the Newtown offense, and, in the minute left before the end of the third quarter, Timo Rivers scored on a straight shot. So at the beginning of the fourth and final quarter, fifteen minutes left to play in the bright hot sunshine, rare for November in Pennsylvania, the championship game score was 2–2. And the Newtown team was ecstatic.

Julie ran to the other end of the field to change goals, slapping the hands of her teammates as she dashed by them, reaching the goal as the whistle blew to begin the final quarter.

For five harrowing minutes, maybe more, it seemed forever to Julie crouched in the front of the goal, her eyes fixed on the ball, the Doylestown offense scrambled after the ball, keeping possession. There were several aborted passes and two attempts at goals, both from number forty-one and both side kicks, difficult to stop. But Julie caught them.

Julie could hear the screams of excitement from the bleachers, the cheers of "Good save, MacNeil!"

There were three fouls against Doylestown, trying hard to get back their strong lead from the first half. And there was a fight between Timo Rivers and a fullback from Doylestown which ended with both boys out of the rest of the game.

The tension was extraordinary. Julie had trouble catching her breath, grateful when the ball was at the other end of the field even though the Doylestown goalie was stopping every kick.

And then number eleven from Doylestown got the ball, and he was flying toward Julie, through the Newtown offense, deep into the Newtown defense with a straight kick in the air, chest level for Julie, which stung her hands when she caught it and knocked the breath out of her for a moment. But she did catch it. And the Newtown bleachers went wild with two minutes left to play.

The game was at Julie's end then, with one foul on the Newtown defense for pushing and two easy kicks at the goal which Julie stopped. She kicked the second one to Tom Baer halfway up the Newtown side and didn't even see what happened next. So many boys were fighting for the ball and everyone was cheering. But it seemed as if Tom still had the ball, kicking it left of center to Tucker Ryan in a fine pass which Tucker received, taking the momentum from Tom's ball straight into the goal.

In the final play of the game, number forty-one from Doylestown took the ball straight down the center of the field, through the Newtown defense with a hard ground side kick to the goal, and Julie fell on it just as the whistle blew.

Newtown had won the county championship 3–2 over Doylestown.

After the game, after the cheers and hugs and congratulations, the cake and ice cream and popcorn served by the parents on the basketball blacktop, after the awarding of the championship trophy and the handshakes, an exhausted Julie MacNeil went home with her father and Tally.

Benji True hadn't been there for the victory party.

"Eliza took him to the hospital," her father told her. "But he refused to go until the game was over. He wanted to watch you at goalie."

"He thought you were amazing," Tally said.

"He did?"

"You were," her father said.

He was in a very good humor, Julie could tell, and she was pleased with herself, pleased she had made him so happy.

Monk was in the front yard when they arrived, a yellow tennis ball in his mouth, his tail wagging; and the Trues' blue Toyota was parked in the driveway.

"They must be here," Julie said, and she jumped out of the car, excited to see them, excited to see them both.

Benji was lying on the couch in the living room, his leg up on a pillow, his knee in an Ace bandage.

"You were great," he said. "I couldn't believe how good you were. Even the coach said so, and he never says anything good in the middle of a game."

"Thanks," Julie said, flopping down on the end of the couch. "I felt awful taking your place like that."

She leaned over him, checking his knee. "What did the doctor say?"

"Ligaments," Benji said. "Probably torn. I won't be able to do sports for awhile."

Eliza came in from the kitchen where she was cooking something wonderful and sweet.

"We couldn't leave until the game was over, Julie," she said, kissing the top of her head. "You were too good."

Julie shrugged.

"I guess I was better than I thought I would be," she said, moving her head away from Monk, who was licking her mouth.

"I have dinner cooking," Eliza said, "And a yummy dessert. We thought we'd get a movie tonight and have a celebration."

"No picnic?" Tally asked. "I thought we were going to have a picnic."

"A home picnic," Eliza said, returning to the kitchen with Tally.

"So," Benji said. "My lucky soccer ball gave you luck."

"The good luck charm?" Julie reached in her pocket and took out the charm Benji had given her. It was a small soccer ball charm, the size of a dime, with writing on it:

STEVEN TRUE, CAPT.
NEW CANAAN H.S. SOCCER TEAM, 1981.

"Who's Steven True?" Julie asked.

"My father," Benji said. "He won it when he was in high school, and he gave it to me when I started to play soccer. Like your mother's wedding ring."

"I guess it sort of is," Julie said, taking off her cleats and going upstairs to shower.

It felt normal to have the Trues downstairs, she thought when she got to her room, Eliza cooking dinner for the family, Benji resting on the couch.

"Normal and nice," is what she said to her father when she went into his bedroom to give him back her mother's wedding ring.

"I'm glad you think that, chum," her father said. "So do I."

She handed him the ring. "I was thinking during the game that I could lose it," she said.

"But I want you to have it," her father said.

"It's really mine?" Julie asked.

"It's yours to take care of," her father said. "Just keep it in a box in your dresser."

She went downstairs and slid up to the kitchen table between Tally and Benji, who were setting up a game of Monopoly.

"What movie are we renting?" she asked.

"*The Princess Bride,*" Tally said.

"I don't want that one," Benji said.

"I want *Raising Arizona,*" Julie said.

"I hate that," Tally said.

"We should rent one none of us has seen," her father said, sitting down beside Julie at the table. "Did I tell you Lila called to ask you to come over to play after school on Monday?"

Julie started to say "I can't" because of Tally's dentist appointment and Monk's distemper shots and dinner, but Eliza said she'd be happy to take Tally and Monk where they had to go, and cook dinner so Julie could go to Lila's for the afternoon.

"I'm going to be working half-time," Eliza said. "So I can be free in the afternoons."

"Then maybe I will go to Lila's," Julie said. "I haven't been over there to play at the barn for a long time."

And she settled into the chair next to her father, leaning into his long comfortable body with a sense of happiness she did not remember feeling for a long time.

"We're getting to have a really big family," Tally said, full of pleasure. "Right Julie?"

"Right," Julie said. "We really are."

***

<u>About the Author</u>

Susan Shreve has written many popular novels for young readers, including *Lucy Forever & Miss Rosetree, Shrinks,* which won an Edgar Award from the Mystery Writers of America; and *The Gift of the Girl Who Couldn't Hear,* a *Booklist* Editors' Choice. Both are available in Beech Tree paperback editions, as is *The Bad Dreams of a Good Girl.* Susan Shreve lives with her husband in Washington, D.C.